For Christopher, Pierce, and Claire—may your kindness and
confidence build the lives you imagine. —E.M.

To my wife, Mar, and our Odile, our little robin.
No doubt seeing you grow up together will be the greatest adventure
that the three of us can live together.
I love you. —A.A.

Published by Yeehoo Press
6540 Lusk Blvd, Ste C152, San Diego, CA 92121
www.yeehoopress.com

The illustrations for this book were created in water color.
Edited by Molly Yao Shen.
Supervised by Luyang Xue.

Library of Congress Control Number: 2022943132
ISBN: 978-1-953458-48-3
Printed in China First Edition
1 2 3 4 5 6 7 8 9 10

OPAL'S SPRINGTIME Birdhouse

Written by Emily Matheis

Illustrated by Albert Arrayás

YEEHOO PRESS

Opal flits with excitement.
It's time for the final contest at
Young Carpenter's Camp!

She **tap-tap-taps** her lucky
nut and bolt in her pocket,
ready for the challenge.

"Campers will vote for their favorite birdhouse!" Counselor Encino says. "Spread your creative wings!"

Imaginations buzz as campers fly into action.

With her eagle eyes, Opal spots glitter and glue, paint and pom-poms, cans and cartons.

She **tap-tap-taps** her lucky nut and bolt in her pocket as ideas soar through her mind.

Damien uses aluminum foil that reflects the morning sun. "Rain will **_pitter-patter_** off my roof!" he says. Opal nods, but she's unsure.

"Mine will have a **_creaky-squeaky_** landing pad," says Meera.

Opal's eyes dart to where the

cling-clang-jingle-jangle

is coming from across the room.

"Birds will hear my birdhouse's doorbells!"
Simon says.

"Sounds fancy," Opal says.

"It's fun and creative!" Damien repeats from
the contest poster.

Opal wonders if shiny roofs, neon puff balls, and ringing bells make the best birdhouses. She crunches another idea into a ball as her excitement slips.

That afternoon, Opal flips through the books that the counselors have left on the table to help with their projects. She twirls her lucky nut and bolt as she learns something new.

Hummingbirds are small
enough for birdhouses, but
they nest on tree branches.

Some owls live in barns, but that is too big for Opal
to build. *Is a barn a birdhouse if a bird lives inside it?*
she wonders.

Ostriches nest right on the ground without any shelter!

Is that still a house?

Other campers have started building their creations, but Opal is still unsure where to start.

"I'll build a birdhouse for the bird I want outside my cabin window," Opal says to herself.

Two pieces of wood for a roof, more for walls. Nails and screws.

Bang! Whack! Whirrr!

She puts the pieces into place. "Just right!" Opal says.

She reaches into her pocket for her lucky nut and bolt,

then attaches them as a perch.

Her confidence soars.

On contest day, Opal is happy as a lark, waiting for the final voting results.

She holds her simple and sturdy birdhouse on her lap.

When Counselor Encino waves the blue first-place ribbon in her hand, Opal sits proud as a peacock.

"The campers have chosen Damien's fun and creative birdhouse as the winner! Congratulations!" says Counselor Encino. Campers squeal, giggle, and clap for him!

Opal's heart dives. Tears rim her eyes. Her claps make no sound.

Opal flees to the cabin with her spirit clipped but determined. *Maybe something will move in*, she thinks and hammers her plain birdhouse to a tree.

Nothing **buzzes**, **hisses**, or **ka-pows**.

Nothing **glitzes**, **flickers**, or **shimmers**.

Her confidence cages inside her again.

"I was sure my house was right for a bird," she cries.

"But it wasn't fun or creative, so I lost."

Opal throws her participation ribbon as far as she can.

It floats to the ground.

A streak of blue whispers by, but Opal doesn't see.
A **scritch-scratch** echoes in the woods.

Damien gasps. "Look at that!" he says.
"I can't believe it!" Simon says.

A bluebird flies
across the yard,
grabs Opal's ribbon,
then goes inside her
birdhouse.

"It worked!"
Opal says.

Good
Effort

"Which birds moved into your birdhouses?"

Counselor Encino asks on the final day of camp.

"No birds even came close to it,"
Damien says.

"Mine either,"
Meera says, shrugging.

"I don't think they like my
doorbells," Simon says.

"What about your birdhouse, Opal?"

"A bluebird moved in!" she says. Her smile beams as campers flock to her.

"Even though your birdhouse was plain," Simon says.

"And bland," Damien adds.

"And didn't make any sounds," says Meera.

Opal stands tall.

"It's just right for a bluebird."

BIRD HABITATS
from around the WORLD

South American Rufous Hornero

These birds build mud homes with clay and vegetation. They're sometimes called red ovenbirds because their nests look like ovens!

The Bald Eagle

Bald eagles build their nests in the tops of trees, using sticks and twigs to make a platform. These nests can be six feet wide and six feet tall, and they are so big—a person can lay down inside!

The Bowerbird

Bowerbirds build beautifully decorated structures to attract mates. They use sticks as well as colorful materials like berries, feathers, shells, and other items that are bursting with color.